AF484441

For matters of military secrecy and operational security for the special operations members, most details won't be mentioned in this book.

This book is a work of fiction. Names, characters, places, and incident either are the product of the author's imagination or, if real, used fictitiously.

US Marine Diaries

Rick Ryan

<u>Prologue</u>

March 15th 2022 – US Marine forward base in Ukraine

In a US Marine forward base in Ukraine, a female US Marine in her middle 20s with dark brown hair and light blue eyes was sitting on a makeshift stool made up from an ammunition box and some wooden planks bolted on it. The US Marine's name was Haiden Zimmerman. She was there in the desert, returning from a boring patrol in the eastern part of Ukraine.

Just as she was thinking of her patrol, she felt something in her pocket before touching it. As she realized what the object was, Haiden took a notebook out of her pocket. On the cover was written 'Zimmerman Family Diary. USMC.' Sensing this diary had something special in terms of content, she opened it and saw a first part, tittled 'My war in the Pacific in 1942-1945 by Tom

Zimmerman.' Alongside it was a picture of Tom, who had brown hair and blue eyes at the time.

Haiden then turned this page and saw it was the first chapter of her great-grandfather's war. Knowing she could learn plenty of things by reading those pages, Haiden decided to begin reading this diary, which she now understood was passed from one generation to another in her family.

Haiden then began silently reading the first lines which were, 'August 7th 1942. We just landed on an island named Guadalcanal. We had spent the previous six months on the defence. Now we're going on the offense.'

Chapter 1

August 7th 1942

Guadalcanal, Solomon Islands

It was August 7th 1942 and then-US Marine Private Tom Zimmerman, who had the same hair and eyes as Haiden, had landed on the island of Guadalcanal alongside other US Marines from the first wave. He was quite surprised by the absence of Japanese resistance, since he and others were told Japanese troops being fanatical soldiers willing to die for their emperor Hiro-Hito. But the first US Marine injured on the island had actually inadvertently cut his finger while opening a coconut with his machete.

Tom and the others then saw the second wave coming ashore before his Captain appeared. Tom turned around and saw the officer taking his M1928A1 Thompson machine gun before arming it.

'Okay, Marines. Let's get to this motherfucking Tojo airfield. We got a job to do right now.' The Marine Captain yelled.

With that, Tom and the other US Marines from his company took their equipment before getting ready for combat. Just as he put his M1 helmet on his head, Tom picked up his Springfield 1903A3 bolt-action rifle and briefly checked to see if it was armed. The rifle had its five bullets in the magazine and the safety off, prompting Tom to close the bolt before taking the rest of his combat load. Just as he was now ready, Tom Zimmerman followed his captain and the others at the start of the column of walking US Marines.

After walking for a while, Tom and his company stumbled on six dead US Marines, who had been tortured, decapitated and disposed off by a tree stump by the Japanese troops on Guadalcanal. Seeing this, Tom swore to himself never to take any Japanese prisoner.

'Motherfuckers. They kill any prisoner they take.' A US Marine swore.

'Yeah. I'll smoke anything looking like Tojo.' Tom concluded.

Just as Tom said these words, he and the others saw the airfield and began searching for any Japanese stragglers in the area. Surprisingly, Tom saw there were no Japanese items, minus for some bags of rice and bulldozers. Tom saw the bulldozers and knew these Japanese machines could be put to good use, since he saw the airfield wasn't ready yet.

Some US Marines from the freshly-arrived second wave then began manning the bulldozers as Tom and the rest of the company move away and dug trenches around the airfield, anticipating any Japanese attack.

Meanwhile, the third and fourth wave had began entrenching themselves near Alligator Creek and the Tenaru River just in case the Japanese would launch an attack there.

'Hey, guys. I bet you all Tojo will attack tonight. I read that Tojo's favorite time to strike was at night, so I tell you this.' Tom told his brothers-in-arms.

'Shut the fuck up, Zimmerman. Those fucking holes ain't gonna dig themselves.' The Marine Sergeant ordered.

Tom obeyed and kept digging his hole, knowing what his sergeant just told him was true at the moment. The young man knew what he would do if he was the Japanese, since he did hear about the Japanese's skills in jungle warfare and fierce banzai charges.

March 15th 2022

In the present time, Haiden had just finished reading this first part of her great-grandfather's chronicles of World War 2 in the Pacific islands. She now felt closer to her great-grandfather Tom, who had been to war before Haiden joined the US Marines in July 2021.

Deciding to know further of her great-grandfather's war, Haiden decided to skip one page and turned it to see another part of the chronicles.

Chapter 2

August 1942 - Guadalcanal

In August 1942, a mere few days after the US Marines landed on Guadalcanal, bad news hit the ground troops, including Tom. The US fleet surrounding the island had been hit hard, causing four US cruisers and two Australian ones plus one American destroyer being sunk. This forced the support fleet anchored in the straight of water named The Slot to withdraw to Australia, where the fleet was being repaired while reinforcements were heading for New Zealand.

But that night, Tom and his company were reassigned to the Tenaru river to relieve the malaria-stricken Marines there. As Tom was on watch duty, he thought he had heard something. Aiming his Springfield M1903A3 rifle at the opposite bank of the river, he was suddenly surprised to see a white flare emerging from nowhere, revealing Japanese troops.

'Japs ! We got Japs on the other side !' Tom yelled, alerting the others.

The other US Marines, including Robert Leckie and Lew Jurgens, then swiftly pointed their rifles at the other side of the Tenaru river. Suddenly, they heared Japanese troops yelling out their, 'Teno Heika Banzai' war cry before 1st Lieutenant Hugh Corrigan fired his M1928A1 Thompson, followed by Leckie and Juergens opening fire with their Browning M1917 machine gun. Tom then opened fire with his Springfield M1903 rifle, killing one Japanese soldier before rearming his rifle while many more Japanese fell dead before Leckie and Jurgen's machine gun.

1st Lieutenat Corrigan then shot two Japanese with his Tommygun before pointing it at two other flanking Japanese, killing them with a short burst from the machine gun. Tom then spotted another banzai charger who had a Hinomaru flag tied to his Arisaka rifle. The US Marine then shot the banzai flag bearer in the head, killing this guy instantly before cycling another .30-06 round in the chamber of his Springfield rifle. Tom then sighted a Japanese officer and shot this guy in the throat, mortally wounding this Japanese before he collapsed forward. Tom then cycled another round in the barrel of his rifle before shooting another Japanese soldier dead.

As more and more Japanese charged, they got killed by Tom and other US Marines entranched at the Tenaru river before the sun began rising over the horizon.

A few minutes after sunrise, Tom and the other US Marines saw all of the Japanese bodies all along both the Tenaru river and Alligator Creek. Tom saw the Japanese dead laying all over the place and discovered what it was to fight a fanatical enemy on land.

Just as Tom was searching a dead Japanese, he heard an explosion and turned around to see two US Navy Corpsmen and a dead Japanese blown off by the latter's grenade. A shocked Tom then took his bolt-action rifle and aimed it at incoming Japanese. Tom then killed one Japanese before Leckie and Juergens mowed the others down with their M1917 machine gun.

Just then, a single Japanese soldier began picking a tantrum while other US Marines were shooting him to make fun of that Japanese. After unbearable minutes of psychological torture, Tom saw Leckie taking his Colt M1911A1 pistol and shooting the Japanese dead before this guy slumped backwards into a pond.

After the brief but bloody battle, Tom and his company were then relieved by another US Marine company, allowing Tom and his comrades to go back to the airfield.

Once they were at the airfield after hours of walking in the jungle, Tom saw Colonel Lewis 'Chesty' Puller coming by them with his men, among whom John Basilone.

'Sir, where are you going ?' Jurgens asked Colonel Puller.

'Tokyo. Do you wanna come with us ?' Puller replied.

'No thanks. We're good here.' Tom politely answered.

With that, Tom saw Puller and his men march away from the airfield to the battlefield.

March 15th 2022

Back in the present day, Haiden realized her great-grandfather must have seen many horrors during the early days of the Guadalcanal campaign.

Haiden then turned other pages of her great-grandfather's diary, since he wasn't present during the slaughter of 1,000 Japanese by Colonel Merritt Edson neither did Tom witness John Basilone halting a whole 3,000

Japanese soldiers all by himself for three days and two nights.

Haiden did get taught how John Basilone exterminated a whole Japanese battalion on Guadalcanal by using machine guns, his own handgun and finally a machete. The young female US Marine also got taught how Colonel Edson and his 300 men stopped an entire 1,000 Japanese banzai soldiers.

But Haiden then kept reading her family's diaries. Then, she discovered her great-grandfather wrote very briefly about his rest in Melbourne.

Chapter 3

January 1943 – Melbourne

In March 1943, Tom and the US Marines from the 1st Marine Division had been relieved from duty in Guadalcanal and were now in Melbourne. Much to Tom and the others' relief, like Sid Phillips or Lew Juergens, the ship was going to bring them in Australia for some well-earned rest while the US Army was battling the rest of the Japanese garrison on Guadalcanal.

As soon as the ship entered the harbor, Tom rushed on the upper deck to see civilians cheering the US Marines and hailing them as heroes for stopping the Japanese forces on land battles. Tom felt as if he should never had this hero's welcome since he saw a lot of his friends dying on Guadalcanal.

But Tom didn't have time to say anything that the ship was already moored at the docks before the crew opened the gates of the ship while harbor workers were mounting gangplanks on the sides of the ship for the US Marines to disembark. Tom then followed Juergens, Leckie and Phillips before going alongside the safety fence while the crowd was cheering them. But Tom wasn't in a good mood, since he was frowning in the face of the civilians while the others of his company were smiling at the crowd.

'Hey, Zimmerman. Why aren't you smiling ? Try to hook girls up !' Sid Phillips stated.

'I'm not in the mood.' Tom said.

Sid Phillips then shook his head as he and Tom walked on the jety to the exit, where they entered another area of the harbor before going into a bus. Right after seating in the bus, Tom fell asleep as the bus drove towards the stadium where the US Marines would be temporarily housed while waiting for another combat at another location of the Pacific islands.

Present day

In the present day, Haiden realized what it was to have some rest during wartime. The young female US Marine then saw several US Marines passing by her before closing her family's diary while inserting a marker on the part she would have to read later.

Haiden then put on her equipment and M27 rifle before following her fellow US Marines to a truck, which would take her and the others to their patrol area within Ukraine.

Once in the truck, Haiden then took her family's diary before reading the part of her great-grandfather's stay in Melbourne.

<u>Chapter 4</u>

Melbourne, January 1943

In Melbourne, Tom had already spent forty-eight hours in the city and he almost didn't do anything while his brothers-in-arms were enjoying their temporary stay in Australia by hooking up with young women and drinking – lots of – alcohol. Tom also knew he and the other US Marines were in a place akin to paradise, where war was miles away.

But Tom couldn't help but think of his own death, one day or another. Tom also didn't know where he would die, except it could be somewhere in the Pacific Ocean. The young US Marine then sat alongside Sid Phillips in a park but was quickly distraught, since Phillips was too busy relaxing to talk to Tom.

Tom then saw a Marine military policeman stopping his jeep before coming towards them. Tom and

Phillips stood up before saluting the MP.

'Right. You are to report to your CO at 12:00 tomorrow.' The MP announced.

With that, Tom and Phillips walked away as the MP got back in his jeep. Tom and Phillips then went to their barracks to prepare to go to war for a second time.

Present day

In the present day, Haiden turned another page and silently read it before realizing the next page was actually a non-written one. Haiden then turned another page, which lead to her great-grandfather's stay on Pavuvu island.

<u>Chapter 5</u>

Cape Gloucester, June 1943

In June 1943, Tom and his patrol, lead by Robert Leckie, were marching through the thick and humid jungle of Cape Gloucester island. But this time, Tom had been re-equiped with a Thompson M1A1 submachine gun to replace the old Springfield M1903.

After a while patrolling, Tom and Leckie came to a stop as they heard voices speaking in Japanese. Looking up a tree stump, Tom realized they just stumbled on a Japanese patrol. Without even waiting for Leckie to fire, Tom bursted out of cover and opened fire with his Tommygun, killing four of the ten Japanese troops. Leckie then popped out of cover and shot the other Japanese troops dead with his own Tommygun.

Just as the duet shot the Japanese patrol dead, they turned around and saw Chuckler Juergens and the others aiming their weapons nowhere in particular.

'We got ten Japanese guys.' Tom said his fellow US Marines.

With this information, Juergens and the others lowered their weapons before Tom, Juergens and Leckie kept patrolling the jungle until they arrived at the rendez-vous point, where they linked up with another patrol.

The following days were so boring Tom found nothing to do, but he however fell sick like Leckied did, forcing Tom and Leckie to be evacutated to the rear.

Present day

In the present day, Haiden now knew her great-grandfather had been sick until July 1944, when the invasion of Peleliu began.

Chapter 6

Pavuvu island, July 1944

After a prolonged stay at a field hospital for a very bad case of diarea, Tom returned to a now-American-occupied Pavuvu island. Once there, he met of course old friends like Robert Leckie, Merriell 'Snafu' Shelton, RV Burgin, Jay DeL'Eau, Lewis 'Chuckler' Juergens or Bill 'Hoosier' Smith. Tom also met new guys he didn't meet prior to the battle of Cape Gloucester but did participate in the battle, like 1st Lieutenant Edward 'Hillbilly' Jones, Captain Andrew 'Ack-Ack' Haldane, James Paul 'JP' Morgan, Wilbur Conley or Gunny Elmo Hanney.

On Pavuvu, Tom also met rookies like Bill Leyden and Eugene Sledge, who would be participating in their first battle ever.

A mere weeks later, the 1st Marine Division was taking part in the invasion Peleliu island, codename Operation Stalemate.

It was in this context that Tom was now in a LVT-4 armored amphibious vehicle alongside Sledge, Burgin and Shelton. Inside the open-top vehicle, it was humid, cramped and uncomfortable since the US Marines were to stay stood for the whole duration of the journey from the boat to the shore. A journey which made them vulnerable to gunfire and artillery shells due to the slow waterborne speed of the LVTs, which could only sail at 9 kilometers per hour.

All of the sudden, as the vehicles came close to the shore, Japanese artillery began pouring shells upon the LVTs, forcing the US Marines inside, including Tom, to keep their heads down. Tom then looked to his right and saw an LVT and it's occupants getting torn to shreds by a Japanese shell. Just to Tom's left, another LVT was blasted, killing all of those inside. Before he knew it,

Tom saw the two US Marines manning the machine guns firing them to hit the Japanese back. Tom saw the Marine in front of Captain Haldane firing the Browning M1919A4 while the one on the left side of the LVT fired the Browning M2 machine gun before the LVT reached the shore.

Tom then spotted everyone disembarking the LVT he was in when the US Marine next to him was killed by a headshot. Haldane then forced Tom out of the LVT, prompting Tom to land next to what remained of a US Marine before Tom crawled to where Sledge was.

'Hey Sledge, ready for this ?' Tom asked.

Sledge nodded as an affirmative answer before the duet ran to nearby trees and linked up with the rest of K Company. Just as they arrived at the rendezvous point, so did Haldane and 1st Lieutenant Hillbilly and Gunny Haney.

'Okay, Marines. We gotta push inland. From there on, it's going to be towards the hills, where we'll be relatively safe. Got it ?' Haldane asked.

Everyone nodded before marching inland with their weapons ready for anything. As the Marines were marching, Sledge spotted something. And that something spat bullets, killing some US Marines and forcing Tom and the others to take cover. Suddenly, one Marine tossed a smoke grenade, enabling everyone to run where the bunker was and be at a safe distance to neutralize it.

Sledge then whispered, 'Burgin ! Burgin ! There are Japanese soldiers in there !'

Burgin then slowly approached the bunker with his M1 carbine shouldered before hearing some voices in Japanese. Tom then checked his M1 Garand rifle before seeing Burgin yell, 'Motherfuckers !' and shoot his M1 carbine inside the bunker, immediately triggering gunfire from the Japanese gunner inside. Tom then aimed his M1 Garand and fired it, injuring the gunner while Shelton and Sledge flanked the bunker. Tom then followed Bill Leyden upon the rooftop where the two of them spotted the chimney. Leyden then motioned Sledge to dislodge the top of the chimney before taking one of Tom's Mk2 grenades and arming it by removing the pin and flicking the safety lever off.

'Fire in the hole !' Leyden yelled before tossing the grenade through the chimney.

A few seconds later, the grenade went off, forcing some Japanese soldiers out of the bunker. Tom shot one of them dead with his M1 Garand before another Japanese tossed a Type 97 hand grenade just before Leyden shot that guy.

Seeing the grenade landed on the rooftop, Leyden yelled, 'Grenade ! Grenade ! Grenade !'

Suddenly, the grenade blew Leyden off the rooftop, injuring him as Tom and the others vacated the rooftop of the bunker. Sledge then went to Leyden's help while Burgin told a Sherman tank where to fire, leaving Sledge barely enough time to cover Leyden before Chuck Womack pointed his M2 flamethrower at the bunker and began incinerating the last defenders inside. Said Japanese defenders came out burning before a US Marine fired his M1A1 Thompson at one of them and killed him. Burgin killed another burning Japanese with his M1 Garand. Tom and many others joined the fray, firing their M1 carbines, M1A1 Thomspsons and M1 Garands at the other defenders before Sledge's eyes.

Tom didn't hesitate to bash a burning enemy's head with the buttstock of his M1 Garand rifle.

A little later the same day, Haldane called all of the company for a quick brief about the tactical situation.

'Okay Marines. Here's the situation. The only way to silence these heavy guns is to those hills. And the only way to those hills is across this airfield. Now let's move.' Haldane ordered.

With that, Tom and the whole of K Company went to charge the airfield while Japanese mortars kept bombing them. Tom witnessed several US Marines getting blown in half or getting a limb blown apart. Tom also ran by Leckie, who was searching for a Corpsman to take care of Hoosier, who got badly injured. Just then, Leckie also got injured by schrapnels while the others kept running to a thick wall, from where Tom witnessed Jay DeL'Eau fired his M1A1 bazooka launcher at a pillbox, taking out it's occupants.

A while after Sledge, Burgin and Shelton sat their M2 mortar, they began pouring fire on anything sheltering Japanese soldiers. Suddenly, Tom saw something he hoped not to see.

'Shit, Jap tank. A Ha-Go with infantry escort !' Tom reported.

Haldane caught Tom's report and ordered everyone to fire anything they had at the tank. Tom fired his M1 Garand at the Japanese soldiers who were running on the sides of the road leading to the Marines' position while Sledge, Burgin and Shelton's mortar shells obliterated many more IJA troops.

Suddenly, the Ha-Go tank was immobilized by a rocket fired from a M1A1 bazooka before Tom saw that Japanese tank getting destroyed by a Marine Sherman tank with infantry escort, who didn't hesitate to turn their attention to the still firing stragglers and either shot them dead or obliterated them.

March 15th 2022

Haiden turned another page of the Zimmerman family diary, she saw what came next.

<u>Chapter 7</u>

Peleliu, August 1944

One month after landing on Peleliu island, K Company, including Tom, were tasked with taking the hills of Peleliu. While marching to battle with Captain Ack-Ack and 1st Lieutenant Hillbilly on the lead, Tom and the others met Chuckler and even Chesty, who were all dirtier than Sledge, Burgin, Shelton and Tom combined. Some of Chesty's Marines were also limping, showing they had hard times up there, especially since they fought on a hill named The Point and on Umurbrogol Ridge, knocking out Japanese coastal guns and radio stations but taking severe casualties in the process.

'Poor guys.' Tom commented, remembering the 5th Marine Regiment was attacking Ngesebu island at the same time.

A US Marine then replied, 'You said it bro. Ngesebu was a cakewalk compared to the ridges.'

The march was then earily silent for the next few hours it took for them to walk there.

A few hours later, Sledge, Burgin and Shelton set up defensive positions while Tom scouted for Japanese fortified position. But the Japanese were so good in camouflage and concealment Tom had to use his binoculars to spot the bunkers. Suddenly, he heard a bullet hit a rock in front of him and realized it had to be a sniper. Tom took cover before taking a wooden board he brought with him and rose it. The Japanese sniper obviously couldn't resist such a tempting target and fired at it, helping Tom know the shot came from the hill in front, aka Bloody Nose.

Tom then emerged from the rocks and fired his M1 Garand rifle at the

sniper, silencing him once and for all
since the sniper was actually killed.
Soon, Ack-Ack and Hillbilly came
followed by Snafu, Sledge and
Burgin.

'I was scouting for Japs when I was
fired upon by a sniper. The fucker's
dead right now.' Tom explained.

'Nice job kid. Nice job.' Ack-Ack
congratulated.

With that, Tom and the others went
back to K Company before going
into battle. And Tom's battle lasted
until mid-October 1944, claiming the
lives of Hillbilly, Ack-Ack and so
many more US Marines before the
Army finally relieved them, allowing
the 5th Marine Regiment to return to
Pavuvu.

As Tom and his comrades returned to
the airfield, many around him,
Sledge, Burgin, De L'Eau and Snafu
were either having a hard time
walking or limping. Tom had to help
a fellow Marine who was badly
injured by a shot at the right ankle.

The Army reinforcements looked in disbelief as the Marines limped back to the ship taking them home to Pavuvu.

In early November 1944, Tom and the rest of K Company arrived in Pavuvu, where they were welcomed by new officers and new Marines, none of whom knew why they were looking at anyone and anything without saying a word.

A new commander, 1st Lieutenant Mac, then spotted Tom and Sledge looking at nurses and said, 'Now that you guys had your have-seen, why don't you keep moving on ?'

But Sledge and Tom looked at Mac with pain in their eyes. And Mac understood what they had been through. Little did everyone know they would through much worse.

Present day

Haiden now fully came to realize
what her great-grandfather had seen
in terms of horrors and bloody battle.
But she also knew Peleliu was going
down in history as a costly mistake
for the Americans. But Haiden turned
her family's diary to the next battle
involving the 1st Marine Division :
Okinawa.

Chapter 8

April 1945

In April 1945, Tom and the other men from the 1st Marine Division were tasked with taking the northern half of an island named Okinawa. The first weeks of fighting at the northern part of the island were favorable to the US Marines since the 1st and 6th Marine Divisions invaded that part of the island in just three weeks. Tom was among the US Marines walking towards the Motobu peninsula at the north east of Okinawa. Tom had witnessed the brutal resistance of the Japanese troops, forcing the Marines to shoot them all dead. In the meantime, Tom and the 5th Marine Regiment learned of President Roosevelt's demise. But the operations resumed as soon as the scouting elements reached Cape Edo. Tom and the 5th Marines also participated in the destruction of the pockets of resistance on the Motobu peninsula.

But Tom and the rest of the 5th Marine Regiment also had to reassure the frightened Japanese civilians who thought the Marines would catch, torture and dissect them alive. But Tom proved not to be a bloodthirsty monster when he spotted a couple and their children begging for life. But instead of shooting them with his M1 Garand, Tom gave them sweats and water. Tom also saw the disillusioned civilians realizing the US Marines, whom they learned to despise, were helping them to have a normal life by building wooden houses, providing food and water and by giving these civilians some basic furniture.

From Motubu, Tom and the other Marines witnessed the hard fighting on the island of Ie Jima.

May 1945

But Tom didn't have much time to interact with civilians when the US Marines were asked to relieve the

27th Infantry Division, the 96th Infantry Division and the 7th Infantry Division all of which had been depleted by the fierce fighting on Kakazu ridge.

Just as they arrived, the 77th Infantry Division began violently assault the Machinato line with some help from the 1st and 6th Marine Divisions. Tom was among the Marines who had to fight in the mud and drenched cliffs of Okinawa.

'Shit ! Tojo's got good leader ! I heard the guy was named Mitsuru Ushijima !' Tom yelled at his comrades.

'Yeah. Japs are pretty good in defense. But we're gonna root them out one at a time.' Sledge commented.

A rookie named Peck and another one named Hamm asked in unison, 'Why ? Why don't they give up ?'

'They're raised with the never give up mentality. Helps them resist our advance. And we gotta kill them one after another.' Tom replied.

Just as they reached a nearby ridge, Tom and his fellow Marines, led by Lieutenant Mac, established a line of defence on the cliffs and the ridgeline.

Sledge suddenly heard some Japanese banzai chargers yelling while charging at the Americans. Sledge dropped his mud-soaked rifle while Tom did the same. Sledge took a nearby M1 Garand while Tom took a nearby M1 carbine before they and their fellow Marines aimed their weapons at the chargers.

'Wait. Wait til they're close.' Sledge said to Hamm.

Just then, the chargers were close enough and Sledge fired his M1 Garand, followed by Hamm, Tom and the others, who quickly gunned the Japanese soldiers down.

'Cease fire ! Cease fire !' Lieutenant Mac ordered.

But Sledge took his Colt M1911A1 pistol and killed the last of the chargers with it. Mac then promptly said in front of Tom's eyes, 'I told you to cease fire and you're supposed to be observing ? I see you with a fucking sidearm !'

'We were sent here to kill Japs weren't we ? What's the matter what weapons we use ? I could have used my fucking hands if I had to.' Sledge told.

Tom and Mac saw Sledge walking away before walking away. And the two of them knew the battle was far from over, since many IJA soldiers died. On the same day as Nazi Germany surrendered.

Tom and his fellow US Marines were indifferent to the announcement of the 8th May victory in Europe and had to fight hard while also sheltering civilians who were rushing to the Americans' position. Tom had to give them sweats and water before gunning down the IJA soldiers on the island.

After a while fighting the same high-pitched attrition battle, Tom and his fellow Marines were involved in the battle for Naha. Tom and the Marines helped the US soldiers take the city within 6 days while other troops had to walk in the mud to surround Shuri castle.

Both sides took advantage of the lull provided by violent storms to settle in for their next move. But this also allowed Tom and the US Marines to take Shuri castle on the 29th of May. But in June, the weather was much better and Tom was once again part of the operations on Okinawa.

June 1945

Tom then witnessed the rapid advance of the 5th Marine Regiment towards Mabuni ridge, still held by the IJA. Just as Tom and the others reached the hill, they were relieved by the newly-strenghtened 6th Marine Division, which took over the operations and conquered Mabuni Ridge.

The 5th Marine Regiment took a well-earned rest at the rear of the battlefield. But the death of General Simon Bolivar Buckner ultimately fired the troops up since the Marines and GI's took the rest of the island by June 22nd 1945.

But Tom's war ended on August 15th 1945 with the unconditional surrender of Imperial Japan following both the two nuclear bombings of Hiroshima on August 6th 1945 and Nagasaki on August 9th 1945 and the Soviet invasion of Manchuria.

Present day

Haiden now knew what her great-grandfather lived during the Second World War. But as she prepared to fold it, she saw a phrase reading 'This was my war. The next one will involve another Zimmerman. TZ.'

Haiden therefore turned the page and saw her grandfather had written, 'This is my Vietnam War by Sweeney Zimmerman. 1968-1969.'

Haiden, seeing there was nothing planed yet, decided to read this part of her family's diary.

<u>Chapter 9</u>

Vietnam, January 2nd 1968

In January 2nd 1968, Sweeney Zimmerman was a young US Marine who just graduated from boot camp and had been assigned to the 3rd Marine Division and had just arrived in Da Nang.

Sweeney had been assigned to the US 3rd Marine Division after joining in the US Marine Corps at age 18. And Sweeney had become a rifleman, there in Da Nang. And this was his first tour of duty in Vietnam, since he noticed everyone looked at him in a bizarre way.

'You the new rifleman, hey ?' A US Marine asked.

'Yes Why ?' Sweeney confusingly answered.

'Cause, you're totting your M16A1 like a backpack. Don't do it. Tuck it between your canteen and an ammo pouch.' Another US Marine replied.

Sweeney obeyed to these two and did as instructed before letting his arm naturally hang alongside his side. And he was now carrying his M16A1 rifle ready-style since the platoon leader called everyone to arms for another long patrol.

But the platoon leader then said all of the platoon, 'Okay, Marines. Our goal is to patrol the jungle around forty klicks from Da Nang. We will then stay near Hue for the rest of our deployment. Got it ?'

Sweeney and the other Marines then replied, 'Sir !'

With that, he and his fellow Marines packed their bag before boarding the UH-1 Huey helicopters which were to take them to a landing zone where Sweeney and his platoon would start their foot patrol.

Little did Sweeney know he would be part of a larger event of the war.

<u>Chapter 10</u>

Vietnam, February 1st 1968

Merely a month after arriving in Vietnam, Sweeney and his platoon were now among the first US Marines to take part in the offensive to take back Hue city from the North Vietnamese, also known as Vietcong. Sweeney Zimmerman was in the leading position, thus leaving him exposed to sniper fire when he first entered the main street of Hue.

Just after entering the street, Sweeney walked alongside a wall with his M16A1 rifle in hands before stopping at a wall in front of him. Turning around, he saw his platoon running towards another set of walls before seeing a fellow US Marine give him a thumbs up.

Sweeney then looked carefully and saw a US Marine M48 Patton tank waiting for a signal to move in. Sweeney then motioned the tank to move to him, to which the commander put his hand on the radio and told the driver to go forward. The Marine Patton tank then rumbled towards Sweeney's position before stopping. Just then, a Vietcong fighter fired a rocket at the tank from the building up front. But the slopped armor deflected the rocket, allowing Sweeney to pinpoint the gunner's position just as the other Vietcong troops in the same building.

After taking his radio, Sweeney told the tank, 'Enemy contact, eleven o'clock. RPG and AK-47. Fire two explosive rounds.'

'Roger.' The tank commander replied.

Just five seconds later, the gunner fired an explosive round that hit the building, obliterating the Vietcong troops there. The tank then advanced at slow speed, allowing Sweeney and his fellow Marines to follow it.

Arriving at a crossing, the tank stopped and a Marine M50 Ontos tank followed by Marine infantry passed it by before Sweeney and the others followed them. Suddenly, the M50 stopped before firing, blowing up portholes. Sweeney then peaked from the left side of the Patton tank and spotted Vietcong troops. He then fired his M16A1 as fellow Marines had taken cover on the sides of the road and were firing everything they got.

A few seconds later, the building was nothing more than smoking ruins. But Sweeney and the rest of his platoon ran to it before stacking upon the sidewalls and tossing tear gas grenades inside said building. Just after putting their mask on, Sweeney and his fellow Marines entered the building with their weapons shouldered.

Sweeney then stumbled upon a coughing Vietcong and shot this guy dead with three rounds from Sweeney's M16A1. Sweeney then spotted another Vietcong reaching for an AK-47 rifle and shot this guy dead in turn.

Upon killing two Vietcong troops, Sweeney saw his platoon killing the rest of the Vietcong fighters in the building before giving an all-clear for the US Marines below to move. Sweeney understood this battle wouldn't be a cakewalk.

<u>Chapter 11</u>

March 1968

A month after entering Hue city, Sweeney and the rest of his company finally enjoyed a little rest when they suddenly heard that the Marine garrison in Khe Sanh had been relieved by the US Army's 1st Cavalry Division. The Marines in Sweeney's company weren't in a happy mood though, since they also learned via the newspapers that the American populace was now embracing the hateful speech of Hanoi.

Sweeney also got a letter from his fiancée. After carefully reading it, he learned she was dumping him for a peace activist and angrily kicked a dead body. Sweeney then took his Zippo lighter and burned the letter before removing his engagement ring and angrily tossing it in the Perfume River, which by now was filled with burning rubbles and rotting dead bodies.

'FUCK YOU JANE ! FUCK YOU JANE ! GO WITH WHOEVER YOU'RE FUCKING WITH, CAUSE I AIN'T GIVING A FUCK BOUT YA ANYMORE !' Sweeney angrily yelled reffering to his fiancée.

'I got dumped, too !' Another Marine told him.

A third Marine then told him, 'Yeah. We're dumped one after another !'

'Fucking mass media !' A fourth US Marine replied.

Sweeney then stroked his dark brown hair before tearing off a picture of him alongside Jane. Sweeney's light blue eyes then began to slightly water before he silently cried.

A week after being dumped, Sweeney had written a final letter to his ex, stating he would also dump her for what she did him before joining the rest of the battalion for

Operation Napoleon/Saline, an operation bound to kick the remnants of the Vietcong out of the southern part of Vietnam. But Sweeney's company would have to walk into a grassy terrain, meaning tanks would be of great help since the infantry and armor would be working together alongside helicopters and artillery.

Sweeney took his equipment and sat on the engine of a Marine M48 Patton tank before helping some rookies get upon the engine of said tank. Once everyone was settled, Sweeney tapped the commander's hatch twice, giving this man the signal to roll out.

Hours after rolling, Sweeney and the other Marines jumped off the Patton tanks and accompanied LVTP-5s to a village named Dong Ha. Suddenly, one LVTP was hit, forcing everyone to evacuate the vehicles. After Sweeney dismounted the LVTP he was in, he was hit in the arm by a Vietcong-manned RPD machine gun.

Just as a Corpsman came to him, Sweeney took up his M16A1 and fired at the machine gun, severely wounding the Vietcong guy while other Marines helped the ARVN retake Dong Ha.

Despite the Corpsman patching him up, Sweeney was still bleeding and had lost some blood until the corpsman arrived. Sweeney was then evacuated to a medevac UH-1 Huey helicopter before being flown to a field hospital in Da Nang, where he would spend the whole month of March 1968.

Chapter 12

April 1968

After a month in hospital, Sweeney was back in the field. But this time, he wasn't a rookie anymore, since two new guys came into his unit the day he came back to his company.

'I suppose you're the FNGs right ?' Sweeney told the two new guys.

Turning around, the two rookie US Marines saw Sweeney's uniform was pretty worn and he was in a quite battle-weary mood himself. Sweeney also displayed no rank insignia, unlike the rookies who had their rank still sewed to their sleeves.

'First things first. Remove those insignias. Charlie aims the leaders.' Sweeney told the rookies.

These two just starred at him blankly until the Lieutenant told them to do what Sweeney told them. The two US Marines complied without a word before Sweeney nodded to his platoon leader in gratitude.

'Good. Now, welcome to Nam, guys.' Sweeney said before putting a cigarette in his mouth.

The experienced US Marine then walked away, followed by the two rookies, who were also part of Sweeney's platoon. But this platoon was actually a scout platoon, which was in turn part of the 3rd Marine Division in Vietnam.

This time, Sweeney was wearing a brown-dominant ERDL camouflage uniform constrasting with the rookies' olive drab one. He knew he and the others would have to babysit those guys, who basically knew nothing about warfare.

A mere four days after welcoming the rookies, Sweeney was in the field, tracking Vietcong forces in Dong Ha region alongside his company. His lieutenant decided that Sweeney must babysit the two new guys, who were wearing a helmet instead of the wide-brimmed jungle hat he was wearing.

Looking at these two, Sweeney asked them, 'Why the fuck did you have to wear a helmet ? I told you to wear a fucking boonie cover like the rest of us. In case a snake tries to bite you from the top of a fucking tree.'

'Sorry.' The rookies apologized.

'It's fucking late for this.' Sweeney told them.

Just as he refocused on the surrounding jungle, Sweeney and the other Marines heard a sound no one would forget, since it was the sound of someone arming a Chinese-made AK-47 rifle.

Sweeney and the other US Marines then opened fire just as the rookies hid behind a huge rock, completely terrified by the hail of gunfire and unable to fire their M16A1s. By the time the duet opened fire, there were seven dead Vietcong fighters nearby.

Chapter 13

May 1968

A month after welcoming the rookies, Sweeney's 45-man platoon was now understrenghth in terms of experienced Marines, since they had five Marines Killed in Action or KIA, ten wounded in action who were now in the US, twenty sick guys and two Missing in Action or MIAs.

Sweeney himself was by now surrounded by either a few battle-hardened US Marines, among whom the Lieutenant, or raw recruits he and the remaining seven guys had to babysit by telling them to wear their hat instead of their helmet for jungle patrols or by advising them not to display their rank insignia.

The lieutenant then had to explain the rookies Sweeney was now his acting Sergeant, filling the role of a platoon second-in-command. The rookies obviously had to heed the eight battle-weary Marines' orders.

Sweeney and his fellow Marines were now involved in yet another patrol in Quang Tri province but there was a difference with the first time Sweeney came to Vietnam. Indeed, this time, the South Vietnamese TQLC or VietNam Marine Corps was leading the sweeping mission. The platoon was therefore on a support role for the South Vietnamese.

After a two-week mission, Sweeney and the others came back to their base alongside the South Vietnamese, who took over the support base. Sweeney and the other Marines in the platoon were so dirty no one could identify them as Americans until they came up close and personal with the South Vietnamese troops at the base. A few minutes after coming back at the base, Sweeney and the US Marines boarded CH-53 Stallion helicopters which took them back to Da Nang.

This was the beginning of the Vietnamization of the war, which basically meant the US forces in Vietnam were going to pack up and go back home.

After an eerily silent flight, Sweeney and the rest of his platoon landed at Da Nang, where they took a shower and had a real meal after weeks eating canned food which, to be honest, were actually the disgusting C-Rations, consisting of canned beef, canned fish, canned cabage, canned beans, canned spaghetti with meatballs, canned hardtack biscuits with cheese spread, canned fruit preserve, canned appricot, canned fruitcake, canned bread, canned pears and canned chicken. Sweeney and the other battle-hardened Marines despised those rations, only eating them due to hunger.

June 1968

In June 1968, the Vietnam War was at it's highest level in terms of military operations and Sweeney was in the middle of this.

This time, Sweeney was officially field-promoted to Sergeant in the US Marines in Vietnam. But he wasn't part of a regular Marine platoon anymore, since his lieutenant transfered him to a recon squad tasked with deep strike and long-range raids. Sweeney was therefore part of a heavily-armed Marine scout patrol feared by the enemy.

A week after his transfer, Sweeney and his new unit prepared their weapons for combat operations. The pointman was carrying an AK-47 while Sweeney and three other Marines had M16A1s. Another Marine was using a Mossberg 500 while the last two had a M3 Grease Gun each.

After the usual briefing, Sweeney and his men boarded the UH-1 Huey helicopter that was to drop them behind enemy lines at night. And the drop was indeed happening at night, since Vietcong forces didn't expect them to operate at night.

A few minutes after descending from the Huey helicopter, Sweeney Zimmerman led his men through the thick jungles of Vietnam in pitch dark. Their mission was quite simple: find any weapons cache and destroy them as well as collect any enemy intelligence they could find during their patrol. And said patrol started as soon as they stopped at a huge tree in the undergrowth.

'Okay, Marines. We gotta find and collect enemy intel, as well as find and destroy enemy weapon cache. But be aware those fuckers could drag us in a tunnel.' Sweeney warned his men.

The other Marines nodded before Sweeney and the pointman took the lead, followed by the others in the squad. At dawn, the eight US Marines then carefully walked inside a stream they found during their jungle trek by foot.

After wading in the stream for a while, they stopped and went on the opposite bank before seeing four Vietcong troops a mere twenty meters away from them. Sweeney then motioned his men to form a line of fire. The Marines then lined up while observing a distance of ten meters between each men.

As the four Vietcong sentries were finishing their chat, Sweeney yelled, 'OPEN FIRE !'

Sweeney and his fellow Marines then fired at will, leaving no chance for the Vietcong troops standing there since the communists were all dead by the time Sweeney and his men stopped firing and reloaded their weapons.

After a whole two weeks in the jungle, Sweeney and the recon squad had gathered a large amount of enemy intelligence and destroyed thirty weapons caches, thanks to said intelligence. The squad also stole several AK-47s for personal use, since these came in handy for infiltration operations like this.

Chapter 15

September 1968

One month after his transfer, Sweeney was back at the hospital for malaria and therefore missed a lot of action from his squad. But the situation had changed back home since support for the Vietnam War was now dwindling and morale on the ground was at an all time low. Many American service members didn't understand why they were fighting in Vietnam anymore.

Sweeney himself was back in the action with his recon squad, though they now had doubts about why they were still there and only knew there were fewer Americans than a few months ago. The process of Vietnamization of the war was by now starting thanks to the upcoming presidential election.

But this goal was still to transfer the defence responsibility to South Vietnam's own forces so that

American, New Zealand, Australian and Korean forces could withdraw from Vietnam while peace talks were still going on in Paris.

Sweeney and his squad now had the mammoth task of training South Vietnamese commandos. Sweeney and his men therefore wore the same uniform as the South Vietnamese troops they were accompanying. The least we could say was these guys were better off with Sweeney's Marines than with the Army guys who were increasingly left to work with the ground forces of South Vietnam.

Sweeney couldn't stop but blame the press and peace activists around the world for spreading pro-North Vietnam news about the conflict. He mostly blamed the hippies for forcing peace talks and giving a bad image of the military to the population, since his brother wrote him a letter stating the American populace was increasingly hostile to the war in

Vietnam, going as far as hailing Vietcong, aka North Vietnam, as heroes.

'Fuck peace activists.' One of Sweeney's men cursed.

'Yeah. My wife slept with a hairy dude last nigh. We're gonna divorce if I make it through this fucking war.' Another complained.

'Me too, Marines. But for now, we can only hang in and wait for these fucking guys in their fucking negociator chairs to find a fucking solution to this war.' Sweeney concluded.

All of the Marines in the squad hoped this war would come to an end, one way or another. They also hoped South Vietnam could be independant.

But their hopes would be useless as History would prove it seven years later.

Chapter 16

Somewhere in the US, March 1969

A whole year after Operation Napoleon/Saline, Sweeney was discharged from the US Marines and went back home. But his hometown wasn't warm-welcoming anymore.

As soon as Sweeney left the airport, a woman tossed a full beer can at his face, calling Sweeney a child murderer. One man even spat at Sweeney's face before he got in the bus, where everyone booed him until he left the bus at the first bus stop, where no one was here to pester him.

By now, even Sweeney's fiancée, Jane, rejected him, calling him a roughneck and a shame to the United States. As soon as he met his ex, Sweeney stood up and went to her.

Turning around, Jane said, 'Sweeney ?! What are you… ?'

'Yeah. You dumped my fucking ass. But I just want one thing. Take back my childhood stamp collection. If I may.' Sweeney retorted, thinking Jane hoped he would get killed in Vietnam.

But much to Sweeney's surprise, Jane hugged him before letting go and taking something from her satchel. Sweeney looked closely and realized it was his stamp collection.

'Well, thanks. I didn't expect someone who dumped me to be that polite.' Sweeney said taking the album.

'You're welcome. Oh, and don't think I was hoping for you to get killed. I did dump you, but I kept your most precious childhood item.' Jane confessed to her ex.

Sweeney then parted ways with his ex, though not as rudely as he expected. It was actually a quite polite breakup and a very nice thing to do before parting ways. But Sweeney was still sad anyways. Sad because he wasn't welcomed like his father had been after the Second World War. Sad of having no one to take care of him. Sad of having been dumped. But he also felt relieved that his ex-fiancée was still polite with him, though she didn't see her as a war hero anymore.

The following months would be a hard time for Sweeney, since he became an alcoholic man who would struggle to make ends meet, being force to work one menial job after another. That was, until he met Haiden's grandmother, who could see the terrified man behind the scars of the Vietnam War.

Present day, Ukraine

In the present day in Ukraine, Haiden realized that peace activists were not all good people, while not all troops were bad ones. She now knew what she suspected : History was made of shades of grey.

Chapter 17

April 1975

In April 1975, Sweeney was now with his new fiancée in a new home when the two of them watched television. Suddenly, the newsreel footage displayed Marine CH-53 Stallion and CH-46 Seaknight helicopters escorted by UH-1 Huey gunships landing in the courtyard of the US Embassy in Saigon, evacuating as many persons inside the compound as they could. Sweeney's eyes begin to water at the sight of these images. His new fiancé, and Haiden's grandmother Candace, understood that it was Sweeney's sadness of having left friends he made in Vietnam fend for themselves.

Sweeney then saw South Vietnamese helicopters fly towards US warships anchored in the South China Sea, where they landed before being thrown into the sea to accomodate more South Vietnamese refugees fleeing their own country. The Marine veteran and Candace then watched the television screen helplessly, knowing those who remained behind would be caught and treated as slaves by the Hanoi regime back in Vietnam.

After a few days seeing footage of fleeing South Vietnamese civilians crammed in American helicopters, Sweeney and Candace watched the news on TV as these footage displayed the last American helicopter to leave Saigon and switched to footage of Vietcong-crewed T-55 and PT-76 tanks crushing the gates of the South Vietnamese presidential palace before Vietcong troops waved the yellow-star-addorned flag at the top of the building.

Present day, Ukraine

In the present day in Ukraine, as Haiden read the last part of her grandfather's war in Vietnam, she also felt sad for the Ukrainian civilians who had lost everything they had due to Russian dictator Vladimir Putin's madness and megalomanic ambitions of building a new Russian empire at the expanse of human lives.

Haiden also remembered she and the other US Marines from the 6th US Marine Division saw hundreds of thousands of Ukrainian civilians crying after seeing their home reduced to a huge amount of ruins by the Russian forces, who had bombed indiscriminately anything displaying a Ukrainian flag.

But Haiden also saw a note to her, from her grandparents. Looking at it, she saw the note read : 'Haiden, this diary is now yours. You will have to tell your war should you join the US Military. But please, do us a favor : don't hate your enemy, don't hate anyone, especially if they're not involved in the conflict, and don't avenge dead civilians. They wouldn't want you to do it. Grandpa and Grandma.'

But Haiden still had deep resentment towards the Russian POWs captured by either the Ukrainian forces or by the Coalition forces, made up of American, British, Canadian, Polish, Lithuanian, French, German, Dutch, Norwegian, Danish, Estonian, Montenegrin, Latvian, Greek, North Macedonian, Czech, Hungarian, Slovak, Albanian, Spanish, Croatian, Portuguese, Italian and Belgian troops.

Upon shutting the diary, Haiden saw NATO troops and her fellow US Marines feeding Russian POWs before photographing them, since these Russians would be traded with Ukrainian POWs. The young female US Marine then walked past the Russian prisoners while looking at them with a deep feeling of distrust and disdain as she didn't say a word.

<u>Epilogue</u>

US Marine base in Ukraine, present day

In the present day, Haiden now knew a lot more about her family's history. Haiden now also connected the dots as to why her father became a civilian helicopter pilot instead of joining the US Marines, why he wanted her to become a civilian pilot or work for anyone but the US Marines.

Haiden's father wanted her to distance herself with a past she always felt attracted to. Just as she saw empty pages in her diary, Haiden realized it was now her turn to write about her war.

Haiden's war indeed started on March 4th 2022 when NATO and their allies decided to retaliate to the February 24th 2022 Russian invasion of Ukraine by bolstering their troops already based in Latvia, Estonia,

Lithuania and Poland. NATO also based thousands of troops in Romania and Georgia to force Russia to withdraw from Ukraine, which had held on for days after the invasion. Both of these forced Russian High Command to withdraw their forces in Ukraine, Abkazia and South Ossetia before signing a humiliating peace treaty isolating Moscow from the rest of the world. But China was also sanctioned by said treaty for supporting Russia in it's invasion though not officially chosing sides with neither Russia or Ukraine.

Now Ukraine, Japan, Taiwan, the Baltic States, Poland and South Korea replaced both China and Russia as permanent members of the UN Security Council, thus allowing NATO to base troops in Ukraine while Ukrainian gas and oil were now the main energy source of Europe and Taiwan had become the main political, military and trade partner of the US, Europe, the UK,

Australia and Southeast Asian countries.

This also triggered the re-activation of six US Army armored divisions, the 2nd, 3rd, 4th, 10th, 11th and 12th Armored, plus eight US Army infantry divisions, the 5th, 6th, 7th, 8th, 9th, 21st, 22nd and 24th Infantry and the re-establishment of the 11th, 13th and 17th US Airborne Divisions.

The US Marines also reactivated the 5th and 6th Marine Divisions to respond to such events and prevent them from ever happening again while America and her allies restarted the production of tanks, anti-tank weapons, anti-aircraft weaponry, electronic warfare devices, aircraft of all roles and radars of all types.

It was in this context that Haiden Zimmerman was now deployed to Ukraine alongside the 6th Marine Division. They were here to prevent any further warmongering from Russia while also reassuring the Ukrainian population. And Haiden knew that Ukrainian people wanted their nation to join NATO as did Georgia in order to remain independant and free.

While waiting for this to happen, these two countries were now under enhanced partnership with NATO forces. Especially American ones, who were the most heavily involved in helping Ukraine keep it's independance.

Seeing nothing was planned so soon, Haiden then began writing her own chronicles of her own war. She then wrote the words, 'My war in Ukraine for her freedom and independance. By Haiden Zimmerman.'

Aknowledgement: dedicated to the US Marines who served and are serving. Semper Fi.

Dedicated to: Robert Ludlum (05/27/1927-03/13/2001)

www.ingramcontent.com/pod-product-compliance
Lightning Source LLC
Chambersburg PA
CBHW061708130726
47996CB00006B/2206